Postman Pat
to the Rescue

Story by John Cunliffe

Pictures by Celia Berridge

from the original television designs by Ivor Wood

Cartwheel
·B·O·O·K·S·™

SCHOLASTIC INC.

New York Toronto London Auckland Sydney

First published by André Deutsch Limited, 1986

No part of this publication may be reproduced in whole or in part, or stored in a retrieval system, or transmitted in any form, or by any means, electronic, mechanical, photocopying, recording, or otherwise, without written permission of the publisher. For information regarding permission, write to Scholastic Publications Ltd., 7-9 Pratt Street, London N W1 0 AE, United Kingdom.

ISBN 0-590-47098-1 *9L-29%*   *5-3-96*   *Scholastic*   *£2.50*

Text copyright © 1986 by John Cunliffe.
Illustrations copyright © 1986 by Celia Berridge
and Woodland Animations Limited.
All rights reserved. Published by Scholastic Inc.,
730 Broadway, New York, NY 10003,
by arrangement with Scholastic Publications Ltd.

12 11 10 9 8 7 6 5 4 3 2 1   3 4 5 6 7 8/9

Printed in the U.S.A.   24

First Scholastic Inc. printing, July 1993

The day had started cloudy in Greendale, but as Postman Pat and his cat Jess set out along the valley, on the way to the village post office, the sun began to come out. Pat's red mail truck went twisting and turning along the winding roads. He went through Greendale Forest, where all the birds were singing. He went around the sharp corner by Garner Hall, then put his brakes on hard.

There was a big truck almost blocking the road. It was Sam's delivery truck.

"It's going to be a tight squeeze," said Pat. He drove onto the grass at the edge of the road. Sam popped his head around the corner of his truck. He waved Pat on.

"Come on!" he shouted. "You've got plenty of room!" Pat wasn't so sure. He edged slowly alongside Sam's truck.

"Left a bit!" called Sam. "A bit more. Left . . . left . . . right . . .
straighten up . . . keep going, you're OK. Come on, come on . . . that's it."

Pat stopped by Sam's truck and opened his window.

"Hello, Sam," he said. "Thanks for seeing me through. Could you give
Mrs. Atkinson her letters, please?"

"Right-o, Pat. Mind how you go. Cheerio!"

Sam went off with Mrs. Atkinson's letters and groceries. Pat tried to drive away, but the truck didn't move.

"Oh, dear," said Pat, putting his head out of the window. He could see the wheel whizzing around and sinking down into the muddy ground. "I think we're stuck."

He revved the engine again, but the wheel just went in deeper.

"Now we *are* stuck. It's all that rain. It's made the ground muddy."

Sam came back.

"Hello, Pat! Still here?"

"Yes, I am," said Pat. "I'm stuck."

"Don't worry," said Sam. "I'll give Peter Fogg a shout as I go past —
he can tow you out with his tractor."

"Thanks, Sam. Cheerio!"

Pat sat on the wall to wait for Peter Fogg to come. Up on the hillside, he could see Alf and Dorothy Thompson busy with their hay making. He could see the sheep and their lambs running and skipping in the green fields by the river.

Peter came at last. Pat was glad to see him.

"Hello, Peter," he said. "Can you tow me out, please? My truck's stuck in the mud."

"Easy," said Peter. "Sam told me you needed help. I'll just back up."

Peter turned his tractor in at a gateway, then backed it up until it was in front of Pat's truck. Then he got his towrope out.

"Now then — just tie it on there," said Peter.

"Right-o," said Pat, tying the rope to a special bracket under the front bumper. Peter climbed onto the tractor again and started the engine.

"Ready?" he called.

"Yes. All ready," said Pat.

Peter drove slowly forward until the rope was tight. He used more and more power until Pat's truck began to ease out of the mud.

Soon it was on the hard road again. Peter untied the rope. Pat started his engine and waved to Peter.

"Bye! Thanks a lot!"

"Cheerio, Pat!"

Postman Pat was on his way again.

When he arrived at the post office, Mrs. Goggins said, "Morning, Pat. You're a bit late today."

So he told her all about how he had been stuck in the mud and had to wait for Peter Fogg to come and pull him out. She showed Pat the Pencaster Gazette.

"Look," she said, "there's a picture of Major Forbes' bull. It's won first prize in the county show. Isn't it a magnificent beast? Have you seen it?"

"No," said Pat, "and I don't think I want to either."

"There's a letter for the major, so you might meet the bull. Better keep a sharp lookout."

"I'd run a mile if I saw it," said Pat. "Cheerio!"

Pat hadn't gone far when he saw Ted Glen waving to him to stop.

"Somebody's left a gate open," he said when Pat stopped. "I'll bet it's those campers. The sheep have gotten into the clover field. It'll kill them if they eat too much. Can you give me a hand to drive them out?"

"Yes, of course I will," said Pat. "I used to work on a farm when I was a lad. Have they gone far?"

"You can see them up there. They have spread out a bit. We'd better get after them."

The sheep were spread across the hillside, busily munching the clover that was so bad for them.

"You go that way, I'll go this way," said Ted.

"Right!" said Pat.

What a time they had catching those naughty sheep! The sheep ran all over the place. They jumped over walls and gates, dodged around trees and bushes, and hid in the long grass.

By the time Pat and Ted had chased them back into their own field and closed the gate, the men were hot and out of breath.

"*Phew,* that was hard work," said Ted.
"What's that funny noise?" said Pat.
"Oh, no. It's that bull!" shouted Ted. "Run!"

They ran down the steep hill and jumped over the wall at the bottom. Ted yelled, "Ouch!" as he landed with a thump on the grass at the side of the road.

"What's up, Ted?" said Pat.

Ted could not stand up, and his leg seemed to be twisted.

"It's my ankle," said Ted. "By gum, it does hurt! Ouch! I can't get up. I think it's broken."

"Now what are we going to do?" said Pat. "You can't sit here until it gets better. I'd better go and get Dr. Gilbertson from the village. Won't be long!"

Pat drove away in his truck to Dr. Gilbertson's house. He gave the doctor her letters, then he told her about Ted's broken ankle.

"Oh dear, my car's in Pencaster being serviced," said Dr. Gilbertson.

"Then I'll take you in my truck," said Pat.

So Dr. Gilbertson brought her bag and rode in the truck. She sat in Jess's place, with Jess on her knee.

Ted was glad to see the doctor. She soon bandaged his ankle, with quite a bit of moaning and groaning from Ted. It wasn't broken, just badly sprained.

"Try not to put too much weight on it, now," said the doctor.

Pat's walking stick came in handy to help Ted hobble to the truck.
"Thanks, Pat," said Ted.
"You'll have to ride among the letters," said Pat. "Easy, now."
Ted climbed in the back.

Jess rode back again on Dr. Gilbertson's knee.
They took the doctor home. Then they took Ted home.
Ted was glad to get home.
"You all right, now?" said Pat.
"I'll manage," said Ted. "Thanks for helping."
"Cheerio!"
"Bye!"

Pat was on his way again. He still had a lot of letters and parcels to deliver. Along the road, he met Alf and Dorothy on their tractor.
"Hello, Alf!" called Pat.

"Hello, Pat," said Alf. "Thanks for getting the sheep back. It's the same thing every year — gates left open all over — we'll have to have words with the campers, won't we, Dot?"

Pat went on his way.

"What a morning, Jess! Rounding up sheep, dodging a bull, fetching the doctor — and now we're late with all this mail. We'll have to get a move on this afternoon."